For My Mum & Dad,
My Stars!

HAROLD'S STAR

Written and illustrated
by Mez Clark

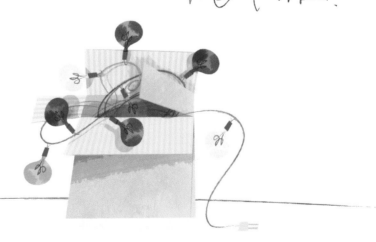

The Sun

Mars

The
Human race
(Earth)

Harold's
Planet

Harold the alien lived in space,
far, far away from the human race.
His home was a little planet, in between the stars,
hidden from all, by the shadow of Mars.

Harold's home was terribly gloomy,
even if it was rather roomy.
Living in the dark was not very fun.
If only, one could see the sun!

Every day he would wave to the ships flying by
and hoped, maybe one might stop to say "hi!"
But they never saw him standing there.
It was pretty dark, to be fair.

This made him ever so grumpy,
so he ate and became rather plumpy!
Feeling sorry for himself,
Harold began to despair,
that he would always live in this shadow
– and it wasn't fair!

But then, Harold decided,
enough was enough,
he ought to stop being in such a silly huff!
The stars that he lived in between,
had always been there and seen.
They shone through the dark and the night
– even in the shadow, they shone bright!

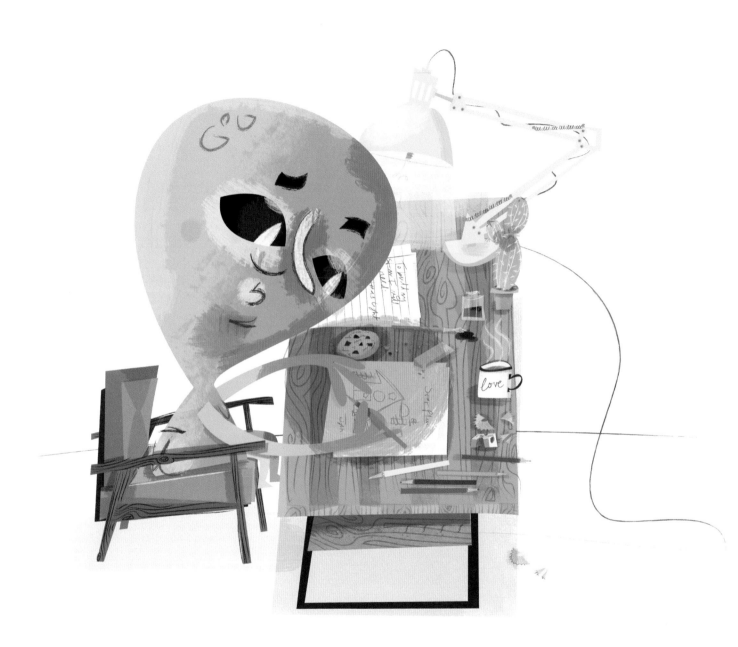

Feeling quite brilliant, Harold had an idea!
"Very clever – indeed", he did believe.
Working through the night, feeling quite inspired,
he planned, making lists of everything required,
to help turn his home into a star,
so that it also, may shine from afar.

He went on the hunt,
through boxes and under his bed,
rummaging in cupboards and then finally, the shed.
Harold collected all he could find
to help transform his little planet into a star
– even if the idea had seemed a little bizarre.

To make his home sparkle and shine,
it was wrapped in fairy lights, to his own design!
He strung them up with string, for that extra bit of bling.
Then for the twinkle, to mimic the glittering stars,
he used silver sprinkles out of tiny jars.

Now, not that Harold had noticed, working so hard,
but ships no longer passed him by.
Although they were still a little shy,
intrigued, they wondered about this sparkling star.
"So bright", they thought, "how beautiful you are!"

At last, work was finished.
Harold's home twinkled, just like a star.
Even Harold had started to glow,
no longer invisible and living in the shadow.
Now, when he waved at the ships flying by,
they would notice him smiling and stop to say "hi!"

Harold's
Star

So, when you see a star at night,
one that shines and twinkles so bright,
smile and wave as it flies by
– not forgetting, of course, to say "hi!"
Maybe it's Harold's star?
Could it be? Sparkling from afar?

The End.

Printed in Poland
by Amazon Fulfillment
Poland Sp. z o.o., Wrocław